ACADEMY OF DANCE

NEW
MOVES

written by
Margaret Gurevich

cover illustration by Claire Almon
interior illustrations by Addy Rivera Sonda

Academy of Dance is published by Stone Arch Books
A Capstone Imprint
1710 Roe Crest Drive
North Mankato, Minnesota 56003
www.mycapstone.com

Library of Congress Cataloging-in-Publication Data
Names: Gurevich, Margaret, author. | Sonda, Addy Rivera, illustrator.
Title: New moves / by Margaret Gurevich ; illustrated by Addy Rivera Sonda.
Description: North Mankato, Minnesota : Stone Arch Books, [2019] | Series:
Academy of Dance | Summary: Gabby is taking the new contemporary
dance class at Ms. Marianne's Academy of Dance, and she quickly bonds with
Sophie, who has transferred into the Academy—but her best friends
seem strangely reluctant to include Sophie in their after-class fun, and soon
Gabby feels torn between her new friend and her old ones, whose
attitude she does not understand.
Identifiers: LCCN 2018037071| ISBN 9781496578235 (hardcover) | ISBN
9781496580214 (pbk.) | ISBN 9781496578259 (ebook pdf)
Subjects: LCSH: Dance schools—Juvenile fiction. | Dance—Juvenile fiction. |
Best friends—Juvenile fiction. | Friendship—Juvenile fiction. | Interpersonal
relations—Juvenile fiction. | CYAC: Dance—Fiction. | Best friends—Fiction. |
Friendship—Fiction. | Interpersonal relations—Fiction.
Classification: LCC PZ7.G98146 Ne 2019 | DDC 813.6 [Fic]—dc23
LC record available at https://lccn.loc.gov/2018037071

Designer: Kayla Rossow

Printed and bound in the United States of America.
2411

TABLE OF CONTENTS

CHAPTER 1

New Class

I place my leg on the barre, bring my chest to my knee, and take a deep breath in as I stretch before my dance class. Chatter outside the studio doesn't distract me. There are always other dancers in the hallway at Ms. Marianne's Academy of Dance.

Today is an especially exciting day at the studio—it's the start of the new contemporary dance team. When I saw the flyer, I jumped at the chance to try out. I've seen contemporary dancers at dance competitions. I love how the discipline combines jazz, ballet, and more.

I'm already on the jazz team, and all dancers at Ms. Marianne's are required to take ballet class. The chance to learn so many different styles of dance and be a part of multiple teams is what makes Ms. Marianne's so special.

I switch sides, lift my right leg to the barre, and grab my toe for a deeper stretch. Someone taps on the studio window. I look up and spot my three best friends, Jada Grant, Brie Benson, and Grace Jenkins. They wave and hurry off to their own classes—ballet, hip-hop, and tap.

Just then a dark-haired girl I don't recognize hurries in and grabs a spot beside me at the barre. She flashes me a friendly smile.

"I'm so excited for this class," she says. "Mr. Viktor was a teacher at my old dance school. Following him here was a no-brainer!"

"No wonder I haven't seen you before!" I say. "I'm Gabby."

"I'm Sophie," she says. "You're going to love Mr. Viktor's energy!"

"Did other students from your dance school come here too?" I ask.

Sophie shakes her head. "No, just me. Contemp is my favorite. I've only been taking it for a year, but I've taken ballet for a few years." She pauses. "It's kind of hard being the new girl. Everyone seems to have their friend groups here."

I nod. I remember when Jada was new here and how hard it was for her. I decide to get to know Sophie and include her in our group.

Just then a tall, muscular man in a navy leotard and black shorts walks into the room. "Welcome to contemporary dance!" he calls. "My name is Mr. Viktor, and I'm excited to be joining Ms. Marianne's as your new contemporary dance instructor. Let's get some basics out of the way. Our class will meet every Monday and Thursday."

One of the dancers raises her hand. "Will we be competing?" she asks.

Mr. Viktor shakes his head. "Not yet. But in three weeks, we'll do a sampling to show the rest of Ms. Marianne's students a variety of contemp moves. This will give everyone a taste of what contemp is and encourage them to try the class."

Enthusiastic voices buzz around me.

Mr. Viktor claps his hands. "Quiet, please. Contemp is about free movement, letting your body do the talking," he says. "I know many of you are new to contemporary dance, so let's start with a move you all should know from ballet, the tilt."

I bring my left leg to my right knee, then tilt my hip as I raise my leg to the side. It's like a standing side leg lift. I make sure my toe is pointed and my leg is straight.

"What do you notice about everyone's tilts?" asks Mr. Viktor.

Everyone scans the room. I notice Sophie's leg isn't as straight as mine, and her foot is flexed. Some dancers' legs are more turned out than others.

I timidly raise my hand. "Everyone's moves look a little different?"

"Exactly!" Mr. Viktor says. "Unlike in jazz and ballet, where each move is precise, contemporary is about feeling the music and doing the moves in ways that speak to you. Let's try the tilt again."

I raise my left leg to my right knee and tilt my hip. But this time when I raise my leg to the side I don't worry about it being perfectly straight or keeping my toe pointed. I focus less on perfect alignment and just do what feels right. The move flows more easily.

"Bravo!" yells Mr. Viktor. "In contemporary each move flows into the other. It's not clear where one move begins and the other ends. I want to see a *fouetté* next."

A *fouetté* turn, or whipped turn, is another move everyone knows from ballet. I stand with my right foot flat on the ground, knee bent. I extend my left leg and whip it around to the side. It grazes the back of my right knee, then moves to the front of the knee as I turn.

"Freer!" says Mr. Viktor. "Melt into the moves. Your body is Jell-O. Watch me."

He demonstrates the turn. His foot is flat like mine, but not as turned out. He extends his left leg and whips it around to the side, just like I did. The difference with Mr. Viktor's *fouetté* is that each step is not distinct. His leg extends and whips in one movement as he turns. It's so quick, it's impossible to tell whether the knee is bent or not.

In ballet class Ms. Marianne is always telling us to imagine strings pulling our arms and legs. Now I pretend I'm a rag doll instead. It feels like a disaster, but Mr. Viktor claps his hands.

"That's it!" he shouts. "Be the wind!"

Sophie and I both bite our lips to keep from laughing.

"Hands curved in front of you . . . and mix the soup!" Mr. Viktor calls. He curves his arms in front of his stomach like he's holding a huge beach ball and moves them in a circular motion.

I follow his movements, feeling a little silly. I hope contemporary dance will feel more natural the more I do it.

"Bravo, ladies!" Mr. Viktor says. "Let's add the needle. Watch me."

He places his hands on the hardwood floor. Keeping one leg on the ground, he lifts the other high in the air behind him.

"Your legs should be in the six o'clock position," he explains. "The leg on the floor is on the six, and the one in the air is on the twelve. You try."

I follow Mr. Viktor's lead, straightening my legs so they look like the hands of a clock and keeping my body in perfect alignment.

"Again! Smoother!" he says.

This time I let my torso flop down and raise my leg into position, not worrying about how straight it is.

"Yes!" Mr. Viktor cheers. "Melt! You are butter!"

I peek at Sophie, who's quietly giggling. I quickly turn away so I don't start laughing.

As class comes to an end Mr. Viktor says, "Practice the tilt, *fouetté*, and needle for Thursday's class. Don't worry about how precise each move is. Focus on flowing from one move to the next."

"That was fun," I say to Sophie as we leave the studio.

"Aren't Mr. Viktor's sayings great?" she replies.

I nod. "Are you butter or margarine?" I ask, giggling.

She taps her lips with her index finger. "Cream cheese," she says finally.

We laugh all the way to the locker room. After getting changed, we grab our stuff and head for the exit.

"I'll see you at the all-team ballet class on Wednesday, right?" I ask.

"Definitely!" Sophie says. She waves as she turns a corner.

The all-team ballet class is a blast. There's nothing more fun than dancing with my three best friends. I can't wait to introduce them to Sophie. I'm sure they'll want to include her too.

CHAPTER 2

INSIDE JOKES

Two days later, Grace, Brie, Jada, and I are at the barre before ballet class. I keep looking for Sophie. I'm sure my friends will love her. Five minutes before class, she rushes through the door.

"You guys, this is Sophie," I say, as she does a mock bow. "She's new here. I met her Monday at my contemporary dance class."

"Nice to meet you, Sophie," Jada says.

"You'll love Ms. Marianne's!" Grace adds.

"Ladies," says Jada, adopting Ms. Marianne's no-nonsense tone, "it's almost time to begin."

Sophie laughs. "I guess all ballet instructors sound the same."

We fool around and exaggerate our leaps and twirls. Suddenly Sophie sways wildly from side to side and sings, "Be the wind!"

I crack up. Grace, Brie, and Jada look confused.

"The wind?" asks Grace.

Sophie and I can't stop laughing. "Mr. Viktor," I finally sputter.

"From contemp class," Sophie adds, still cracking up.

My friends still look confused. Brie looks from me to Sophie then back to me. "I guess we had to be there," she says softly.

Why does Brie sound sad? I wonder. *The four of us laugh about stuff all the time.*

Before I can explain further, Ms. Marianne walks into the studio. Her salt-and-pepper hair is tied back into a tight bun, and a yellow scarf pops against her black leotard. She claps her hands to begin, and we all take our places at the barre.

"*Pliés* first, ladies!" she calls. We all bend our knees and sink down obediently.

"Lovely!" says Ms. Marianne. "Line up for *grand jetés.*"

Sophie lines up behind me. "Your body is Jell-O," she whispers as we wait our turns.

I snort in my attempt to hold in a laugh. Ahead of me, Brie and Grace turn and frown.

Sorry, I mouth, still trying not to laugh. When it's my turn, I leap across the floor, legs spilt.

"*Adagios!*" Ms. Marianne calls as we finish the *grand jetés.*

I bend my leg and raise it behind me. Then I rise to my toes for *relevé.* As class winds down, it starts sprinkling outside. Rain pelts the big picture window in the studio, and Sophie whispers, "Be the rain."

This time I can't hold in my laughter.

"Shhh," Jada hisses.

I blush. "Sorry."

Ms. Marianne gives me the evil eye, and I compose myself.

When class is over, I playfully elbow Sophie. "I thought Ms. Marianne might kick us out!"

"I'm surprised she didn't," Jada says dryly.

Grace wrinkles her nose. "Yeah, you guys were a bit much."

I look at my friends, feeling hurt. It's not like the four of us have never goofed around in class. I was just having fun with my new friend, trying to make her feel more comfortable.

"Were you annoyed too, Brie?" I ask.

Brie shifts from one leg to the other. "It was a little distracting," she says quietly.

Sophie looks away and doesn't say anything. I thought my BFFs would be happy to meet a new friend. But instead they're making her feel unwelcome.

Brie forces a smile. "Who's up for after-ballet pizza?" she asks.

"Me!" says Grace.

"Always," adds Jada.

Grace, Jada, and Brie all glance over at Sophie and me. Sophie swallows and looks uncomfortable.

"I, um, I might just go home and practice some more for tomorrow's class," she says. "We have our sampling in three weeks. I want to make a good impression since I'm new here, you know?"

I feel even worse. My friends' behavior made me feel like Sophie and I did something wrong. I don't want her to feel left out.

"Can I come?" I ask Sophie. "I could use the practice!"

Sophie's face lights up. "That would be awesome!"

Grace heaves her gym bag over her shoulder. "But you *always* come out for pizza after ballet," she says.

"We really need to practice. . . ." I say. "You guys understand, right?"

The corners of Jada's mouth pull up into a strained smile. "It's cool," she says. "We'll catch up with you both another time."

She, Grace, and Brie grab the rest of their stuff and head out, barely saying another word.

"They seemed a little upset," says Sophie when my friends are gone.

I agree, but I don't want Sophie to feel worse. "Nah, they're probably just hungry."

I tell myself the same thing. My friends being upset I chose dance over pizza just doesn't make sense.

CHAPTER 3

Dancing Duo

Sophie rummages in her bag for her house key
and unlocks the door. It's so quiet compared to
my house, where I live with my mom and *abuela*.

"Where is everybody?" I ask.

"My mom's at work, and my dad works the
night shift, so he's still sleeping," Sophie explains.
She hands me a brownie from the plate on the
kitchen table. "Here, my dad made these."

I tear into mine, suddenly famished.

Sophie shoves the brownie into her mouth.
"Oh good, we're not being polite," she says.

I laugh, almost choking. The tension I felt with
my friends disappears.

After we eat, I follow Sophie into her family room. There's a large open space in the middle. "We can practice here," she says.

Sophie rises to her toes and curves her arms in front. She does a *fouetté* in the center of the room.

"Mix the soup!" I call.

She bursts out laughing and loses her balance. "Stop distracting me," she says, still giggling.

"Sorry," I say. "Continue."

Sophie closes her eyes so I won't distract her. I notice how easily she flows from one move to the next—tilt to *fouetté* to needle.

"Your turns are so good," I say. "How do you do that?"

Sophie smiles. "I try to let my body go."

"Like Jell-O?" I joke.

"Mr. Viktor's sayings are silly," says Sophie, "but they're spot-on. The moves don't have to be exact. Just flow from one move to the next."

I try to follow Sophie's advice, moving from the tilt to *fouetté*. I relax my muscles as my leg swings behind me and then out front. I close my eyes and move my torso in the same direction as my arms. For the needle, I let my body relax as I place my hands on the floor and lift my left leg to the ceiling.

"That's it!" yells Sophie excitedly.

I beam. "Let's try it together!"

Sophie and I stand in opposite corners. We raise our legs to the side for the tilt, then twirl toward each other for the *fouetté*.

"We make a good team," I say.

"No doubt." Sophie fist-bumps me.

We spend the next hour practicing. By the time I'm ready to go home, the earlier weirdness with my friends is behind me—almost.

CHAPTER 4

WHAT'S THE PROBLEM?

"How was pizza?" I ask Grace, Brie, and Jada the next afternoon.

"Jada decided to try the jalapeño pie," Brie says, giggling.

"*Big* mistake!" Jada adds with a laugh. "I spit a pepper all over the table and—"

"Sophie made me laugh so hard yesterday, I almost spit out my brownie!" I interrupt.

Jada frowns, but Grace bumps my hip and says, "We missed you."

"I missed you guys too," I say. "But Sophie and I had so much fun."

Brie pauses, then asks, "What did you guys do?"

"Mostly practiced, but Sophie is so great. She's an awesome dancer and—"

"Sounds cool," says Grace, cutting me off.

I frown. What's their problem? I just want my friends to like Sophie as much as I do.

"She's really funny," I continue. That's another thing Sophie and my friends have in common.

"Sounds like it," Brie says quietly.

"Do you guys want to hit the mall this weekend?" Jada asks, changing the subject. "I could use some retail therapy."

"That would be great!" I say. "I'll see if Sophie wants to join."

"Oh . . . I don't know . . ." Jada begins. She, Brie, and Grace exchange a look I can't quite read.

Why do they keep looking at each other? I wonder. *Do they not want to hang out with Sophie?*

I keep talking, hoping to convince them. "Come on. Dance store, food court, window shopping . . ."

"Those *are* my favorite things," Grace says.

I look expectantly at Brie and Jada.

"Let's do it," Brie says. Jada nods too.

Once they get to know Sophie, they'll want to spend time with her too, I tell myself. *She'll fit into the group in no time. I'm sure of it.*

* * *

Saturday afternoon, Sophie and I sit on a mall bench and wait for my friends. "This is going to be great!" I say, trying to convince us both.

"I hope so," Sophie says, looking nervous.

Finally Brie, Jada, and Grace walk in. Sophie's smile pops into place, and I wave to my friends.

"Who's ready to shop?" Jada asks, grinning.

"I'm *so* ready!" Sophie exclaims.

"My kind of girl," says Grace.

I smile happily. Whatever was bugging my friends seems to have passed.

We agree to head to the food court for a snack first, and in a few minutes, we're chowing down.

"Food court lo mein is *the* best," Grace says, slurping her noodles.

Brie wrinkles her nose. "That sound is so gross," she says.

"*This* sound?" I ask, snorting as I eat lo mein.

Sophie laughs. A noodle flies out of her mouth and onto the table. She blushes. "I'm so sorry!"

I put my arm around her. "You fit right in."

Everything is going better than I expected.

"What was your old dance school like, Sophie?" Brie asks, cutting up her noodles into neat pieces and eating them quietly.

Sophie shrugs. "It was a lot smaller than Ms. Marianne's."

"I think you'll really like the classes here," says Jada. "Most of the teachers danced professionally in New York City."

"Sophie told me that Mr. Viktor danced on Broadway!" I gush.

"Cool," says Grace.

Sophie clears her throat. "I like that Ms. Marianne's has so many options. Even the ballet is more advanced!"

At the mention of ballet, Jada perks up. "What were your old ballet classes like?"

Sophie takes a bite of her lo mein. "There were only a few of us with ballet experience. Most of the classes were beginner."

I don't want Sophie to feel like her skills don't match ours. "Sophie is so amazing at contemp! You guys are going to be blown away by our sampling."

I look at my friends, but they don't seem interested in the conversation anymore. I try to think of something else that can involve Sophie. "Mr. Viktor has so much energy!"

"So does my hip-hop teacher," says Brie quietly.

I slump in my seat. *It's not a contest,* I think to myself.

"I'm so full," says Brie, pushing away her half-eaten food. "Do you guys want to hit Dance Till You Drop next?"

"Great plan!" I say, cheering up. "Sophie and I have to shop for our sampling."

I turn to smile at Sophie, but I catch Grace and Jada rolling their eyes. Even Brie lets out a deep sigh. This time I know I didn't imagine their reaction.

Why do they get so annoyed every time I talk about what Sophie and I have in common? I wonder. *Why can't my friends just be happy for me?*

CHAPTER 5

Too Much Contemp

"How great is this store?" asks Sophie when we enter Dance Till You Drop. "I've never been here."

"We come here all the time," Jada says.

"Thanks for inviting me today," says Sophie.

"It was really Gabby," Grace says, avoiding Sophie's eyes.

I shoot Grace a look. *Why are they being so rude?* "Sophie and I are going to look at leotards," I say.

Sophie looks from me to my friends. "Do you guys want to come with?" she asks hopefully.

"I want to look at tap shoes," Grace says.

"Besides, aren't you two shopping for your sampling?" Jada asks.

Brie shoves her hands in her pockets. "We don't want to intrude," she adds softly.

"You wouldn't—" Sophie begins.

"Forget it," I interrupt. I turn away from my friends, saying, "Find us when you're done."

As my friends walk off, I'm speechless. Sophie was trying to be nice, and they blew her off.

"I don't want to come between you and your friends," says Sophie anxiously.

I want to say something reassuring, but it's all so weird. "I'm really sorry. I've never seen them act like this." I hook my arm through Sophie's. "Leotards, here we come!"

I drag her to the leotard section, and Sophie finally smiles. "Oh my gosh," she whispers, holding up a sparkly, rainbow-colored leotard, "is this way too much or is it just me?"

"Be the rainbow," I joke.

Sophie giggles and hangs it back on the rack.

I hold up a leopard-spotted leotard with a fur trim around the neck. "*Purrfect* for teaching dance in a safari," I say.

"Shhh!" Sophie giggles as the clerk glares at us.

We sift through the sale rack, taking turns mocking outrageous designs.

"Wait!" squeals Sophie, holding up a bright blue leotard. "I actually found a good one!"

"Ooooh great color!" I say. "Find one for me."

"On it!" Sophie replies. Suddenly she spots something over my shoulder, and her face falls.

I turn and see Brie, Jada, and Grace coming our way. My heart sinks. The only time I've ever felt this way around my friends was when Brie and I had an argument over a solo. But even then I still had my other friends.

I shift from one foot to the other as my friends approach. "Did you buy new tap shoes?" I ask Grace without thinking.

As soon as the words are out, I regret them. Grace likes to browse the shoe selection here to get ideas, but she can't afford new ones. She and her mom always buy them secondhand.

Grace tenses. "Nothing I like," she says tightly.

"Grace, I didn't mean—" I start to say.

"It's fine," Grace interrupts. Her tone clearly tells me it's not.

I know her irritation isn't about the tap shoes. Grace knows I'd never bring up her money stuff on purpose. It's about Sophie. As usual.

"What did you all find?" Brie asks softly, trying to change the subject.

Sophie holds up a leotard. "Cool, right?"

"Definitely!" says Jada.

"Thanks!" I say happily. "That's what's so great about contemp. We can wear funky things."

Jada bristles. "Unlike boring ballet leotards?"

"You know that's not what I meant!" I protest.

"Let's go outside and work this out," Sophie mutters as the clerk starts walking toward us.

Back out in the mall, Brie says, "I should go. My dads wanted me to be home by three."

"I promised my mom I'd help her around our house," adds Grace.

I'm so mad at all of them. I know it's wrong, but I can't help being a little snarky.

"Fine," I say. "Sophie and I need to practice our contemp moves anyway. Right, Sophie?"

Sophie looks like she wants to disappear, and I regret dragging her into this.

Jada throws up her hands. "There's a shock."

"What's *that* supposed to mean?" I snap.

"It *means*," says Jada, "that contemp is all you talk about. It's contemp this, and contemp that, and everything you and Sophie do together. You even interrupted my jalapeño pepper story to talk about you and Sophie!"

"You're mad about a *pepper*?" I yell. I turn to Brie, who looks like she's going to cry. "Do you agree with Jada?"

Brie nods slowly. "You do talk about contemp a lot." She glances at Sophie. "And it's nothing against you, Sophie. It's just that you two only seem to want to hang out together—"

"We *all* came here together!" I interrupt furiously. "You three are the ones who decided to split from *us* in the store."

Sophie touches my shoulder, looking upset. "I'm going to go."

"But—" I begin.

"I'm going to go too," Grace says.

"Later," Jada says curtly. She and Brie walk away without a backward glance.

In an instant, I'm alone. All I can do is watch my old friends and my new friend walk away and wonder where everything went wrong.

CHAPTER 6

Just Dance

My friends and I don't text for the rest of the weekend. It's just as well. I don't know what to say to any of them. I feel especially awful for putting Sophie in the middle.

On Monday afternoon, I walk into my contemp class, nervous about seeing Sophie. I haven't talked to her since the disastrous mall outing.

As I'm warming up at the barre there's a tap on my shoulder. I turn and see Sophie standing there.

"Hey," she says. "How are you?"

I'm relieved she doesn't look mad. I shrug. "OK . . . I guess."

"That was some weekend, huh?" she says.

I cringe. "I don't know what happened."

Sophie bites the inside of her cheek. "I think I do. Let's talk after class."

Just then Mr. Viktor walks in. "Places!" he calls.

Sophie bumps my hip and grins. "Be the wind," she whispers.

I grin back. It can't be too bad if Sophie is still cracking jokes.

"We have four more classes before our sampling," Mr. Viktor reminds us. "I hope you've all been practicing. Let's review our steps from last week, then add on. Remember—be free!"

I glance at Sophie, and she mouths *free.* I hold in a laugh and try to take the advice to heart.

Free your mind, I tell myself. *Be Jell-O.*

I move my arms in front of me like I'm holding a huge beach ball and loosen my shoulders as I mix the soup. My leg rises to the side for the tilt, then whips back and forward for the *fouetté.*

"The song we'll be using for our sampling is called 'All Together,'" Mr. Viktor explains. "To emphasize the togetherness, I want you to connect to each other on the needle."

I'm not sure what he means by *connecting*, but I like the idea of expressing emotions in the song.

"For the needle, line up with a partner, and lace your fingers together as you lift your opposite legs in the air," he instructs.

Sophie and I partner up to practice the move. Our hands fall to the floor, and we lace our fingers together before lifting our legs into the twelve o'clock position. Lacing our fingers actually helps me balance too.

"Bravo!" says Mr. Viktor. "Now with music."

I close my eyes and focus on the beat as I lift my leg for the tilt. I don't pause as I complete the *fouetté* turn. Then Sophie and I run to each other and lace our fingers together for the needle.

Seeing all the dancers' fingers connected as we raise our legs helps the song come alive, and I understand what Mr. Viktor meant about the moves coming together.

"Beautiful!" shouts Mr. Viktor. "Next we're going to add a layout. This is a dramatic move. As the music gets louder, that's your cue to do the layout. Watch me."

Mr. Viktor replays the song. As the music swells, he brings his left foot forward. His right foot brushes across the floor and off the ground as he arches his back and throws his arms behind him.

When it's our turn to try, I listen for the musical cue. I lift my left leg high off the floor as I arch my back and fling my arms behind me. I melt and imagine the moves flowing into one another. As the music gets louder, and the singer croons about friendship, my body goes limp as it arches backward.

I almost choke up, hearing the lyrics. I hope Sophie really does know what's been bugging my friends.

* * *

"That was a hard practice," I say to Sophie as we gather our things in the locker room.

Sophie nods. "I think our sampling is going to look great, though," she says.

"Definitely!" I think about the song, my friends, and how we love watching each other dance. I wish I could share this with them.

"What's wrong?" asks Sophie.

"I was just thinking about my friends," I admit. "You really know what's bugging them?"

Sophie nods. "I think they feel left out," she says.

"What do you mean?" I ask. "Just because we didn't join them for pizza?"

"That's part of it," says Sophie, "but—"

I throw up my hands. "You and I needed to practice! And besides, the four of us hang out all the time."

"You might be right," Sophie says cautiously. She reminds me a bit of Brie when she's about to bring up something she knows I won't like. "But maybe that's part of why they're hurt. They're used to hanging out with you. And you and I have been talking about contemp *a lot.* . . ."

"They talk about their dances too," I insist. "*They're* the ones who were rude at the mall."

Sophie doesn't say anything else. Instead she focuses on packing her gym bag.

"Are you mad at me too?" I ask. I can't bear another friend not wanting to talk to me.

"Not at all!" Sophie says, looking up from her bag. "I just don't want to come between you all. I'd like *all* of us to be friends."

"Me too," I say eagerly. "They should apologize."

Sophie wrinkles her nose. "Just think about what I said, OK?"

I want to argue about how silly that is, but the look on Sophie's face stops me. Even though I *think* it's ridiculous, I nod in agreement. Then I change the subject. "Want to come over and practice our moves after ballet class?"

"Great plan!" she says. "I want to be as close to perfect as possible for our next class."

"Same," I agree. What I don't say is that the more time I spend practicing, the less time I'll have to worry about whether or not the fight with my friends is really my fault.

CHAPTER 7

My Fault?

"Let's take turns so we can see what the other looks like," Sophie suggests. It's Wednesday afternoon, after ballet class, and we're getting ready to rehearse in my basement. "Then we'll do it together like in class."

"You first," I say.

Sophie moves easily from the tilt to the *fouetté*, her leg swinging behind her knee and then to the front. Without pausing, her palms go to the floor and her leg rises to twelve o'clock for the needle. I imagine the song getting louder as Sophie stands up for the layout. She kicks her leg out in front, arches her back, and raises her arms behind her.

I applaud when she finishes. "That was so buttery!" I tell her, laughing.

"You're up next," says Sophie.

I wiggle my body to loosen up, and Sophie giggles. I tilt my hip and complete my side leg lift, then curve my arms in front of me and whip my leg around for the *fouetté*.

Be the wind, I think as I twirl.

My hands go to the floor for the needle like they have a mind of their own, and then I'm back up, body arching, hands flying behind me for the layout.

Sophie whistles through her fingers. "Wind, rain, we can be anything!"

Just then, the doorbell rings. I rush up the stairs, expecting it to be the pizza my mom ordered, and peek through the window. Brie, Grace, and Jada stand on the other side, looking nervous. My palms sweat as I open the door.

Brie shifts from one foot to the other. "Can we please come in?"

I nod and motion them in. I feel sad at how formal Brie's question sounds.

"We wanted to talk about what happened at the mall," Brie says. "I feel awful."

"Me too," Grace adds quickly.

"Me three," Jada chimes in. "We shouldn't have gotten so annoyed."

I sigh with relief. "I'm so glad you guys feel that way. I don't know what happened. You ditched Sophie and me and were being all snooty and—"

Brie's mouth drops open. "Wait, *we* were being snooty?"

Grace puts her hands on her hips. "It was all *us*?" she says in disbelief.

I give them a confused look. I can't believe they're acting like this is my fault. I thought they were here to apologize.

"Um, yeah?" I say. "You made it clear you didn't want to hang out with us. And any time we even mentioned contemp class you all made faces."

"C'mon, Gabby!" says Jada, exasperated. "It feels like you never want to spend time with us anymore. It's all about Sophie. And all *you* ever want to talk about is contemp—no matter what we're talking about."

What she's saying is similar to what Sophie suggested, but I'm too mad to think straight. "If that's how you feel then go," I lash out. "Sophie is downstairs, and we're practicing our *contemp* moves. I wouldn't want to bore you guys."

Brie's eyes fill with tears, and I feel horrible.

Grace puts her arm around Brie. "Let's go," she says.

Jada looks at me sadly. "Why did we even come over if you can't talk about this?"

I don't have anything to say to that. My friends leave, and I slump down on the floor and put my head in my hands. I hear Sophie coming up the stairs, but I don't move.

"That was a mess," I whisper as she puts her hand on my shoulder.

"You'll work it out," says Sophie.

"Maybe you were right," I say. "Maybe I *did* make them feel left out."

Sophie sits down next to me and gives me a gentle hug. "Think about what I said, but don't beat yourself up," she tells me. "No one is perfect."

* * *

When Sophie leaves, I think about how I've been acting over the the past week. I remember interrupting Jada when she was laughing about what happened at the pizza place. I remember cutting off my friends' stories at the mall with contemp talk.

I didn't mean to be rude—I was just excited to share what was going on with my new friend and my new class. And I wanted them to be friends with Sophie too. But I think about how my friends must have felt when I kept interrupting all their stories with contemp moments Sophie and I shared—moments they were left out of.

They hurt my feelings too. But is it possible they were trying to own up to how *they* acted before I placed *all* the blame on them?

I take a deep breath and whip out my phone to text Grace, Brie, and Jada. Then I grab my jacket. After telling my parents where I'm going, I head out the door.

Sophie's right. No one is perfect. I just hope we can work out all our imperfections together.

CHAPTER 8

APOLOGIES

My mouth is dry, and my heart is racing as I stand in front of our favorite pizza place. I don't know where to start, but when Grace, Jada, and Brie walk toward me, two words immediately spring to mind.

"I'm sorry!" I blurt out. "I'm sorry it seemed like I didn't want to hang out with you guys, and I'm sorry I blamed it all on you when you came over to apologize."

Grace, Jada, and Brie stare at me, surprised.

I bite my lip. "Wait," I say hesitantly. "That *is* why you guys came over before, right?"

Brie recovers. "Totally! It's not all your fault."

I breathe easier.

Jada blushes. "We got a little jealous."

"A lot jealous," adds Grace.

Brie nods. "It just seemed like you only wanted to spend time with Sophie, and since we couldn't talk about contemp with you . . ."

"We thought you didn't want to hang out anymore," Jada finishes.

My eyes widen. "What? That'll *never* happen!"

"But even if we felt left out, we should have wanted to hear about your new class. It's important to you," Brie continues.

"We'll do better." Jada smiles shyly.

"And I'll work on including you all more," I say. "Sophie made me realize I wasn't doing a very good job including you guys."

Grace looks embarrassed. "None of this is her fault. I'm sorry we were rude to her. She seemed really nice at the mall."

"She is!" I exclaim. "That's part of why I like her so much. She's just like us. She's silly and funny and a great dancer."

"Think she'll give us another chance?" Jada asks. "Or at least let us apologize?"

"Definitely!" I reply.

"Do you want to text her and invite her for pizza?" asks Grace.

"You sure you're all fine with that?" I ask.

"She *did* make you think rationally," says Brie with a wink.

I laugh and text Sophie. When she replies *Be there in 10!*, I feel even happier. For the first time in a while, things feel normal.

CHAPTER 9

Home Stretch

"Let's get to work, ladies," Mr. Viktor says on Thursday. "We only have today's practice and Monday's. Then it's showtime!"

Excited whispers fill the room.

Mr. Viktor claps his hands for silence. "Today we'll learn the scorpion pose and illusion. If the latter move is done correctly, it will look like a giant, spinning pinwheel," he says. "Let's tackle the scorpion first. Plant your right foot on the floor and raise your left leg behind you." Mr. Viktor demonstrates as he talks. "Bend your torso forward and reach behind you to grab your left ankle with both hands."

I watch carefully. It's clear you need a lot of flexibility for this move, and I'm thankful for all my ballet stretches.

"Now you try," says Mr. Viktor.

I scrunch up my face and concentrate hard, wanting to do the move perfectly. *I'm a rag doll*, I tell myself as I fall forward and reach behind me to grab my ankle.

"Fabulous!" cheers Mr. Viktor. "Now, for the illusion. Begin in needle position with your raised leg on the twelve. Keep the pressure in your foot, not your hands, as you rotate on the ball of your foot. You want to move in a half circle."

He uses his hands to move halfway around an imaginary circle, but I see his pressure is in his foot.

"Let's try this before we move on to the next step," he says.

I've mastered the needle, so that part is easy. I place my hands on the floor, put pressure on my right leg, and raise my left leg high in the air. I turn, making sure it's the ball of my foot that's moving me in a circular position, not my hands.

"Terrific!" Mr. Viktor cheers. "Now do that again, but move the leg at the twelve o'clock position around with you. Use your hips to rotate your whole body. Watch me."

Mr. Viktor demonstrates the move as he did before, but this time the leg in the air follows him all the way around in a half-circle. When he's done, he's facing in the opposite direction from where he started.

"The goal," he continues, "is to do this without placing your hands on the floor at all. Think of a no-handed cartwheel, but with one leg on the ground and one in the air."

This helps me visualize what he means. I keep practicing, moving my leg faster and faster.

"Line up facing your partners," says Mr. Viktor. "Do your illusions facing each other down the line. And a-one, and a-two, and a-three."

In unison, we bend down and complete our rotations. Mr. Viktor has each group take turns watching the others. Just like he said, with the legs moving, it looks like a pinwheel.

"Fantastic!" he shouts. "We'll run through the routine one more time Monday. But please practice over the weekend as well. It will be fabulous!"

He's right—the sampling will be fabulous. Especially now that my friends will be watching and cheering for Sophie and me.

CHAPTER 10

SHOWTIME

After one final contemp practice, it's showtime. Sophie and I get into position in the largest studio at Ms. Marianne's, along with the rest of the contemp dancers. All the other dancers and instructors are squished into the studio to watch what we've learned. It's not a recital, but I'm still excited to show off my new moves.

Be loose, I tell myself. The music starts, and we pop our hips and lift our legs to the side for the tilt. The music speeds up, and we swing our legs back and forward again for the *fouettés.*

Sophie and I bring our hands to the floor. Our fingertips touch while our legs lift behind us.

Upright again, we form two circles for the layouts. We arch our backs, kick our legs forward, and raise our arms behind us toward our ears.

Melt, I tell myself as I bend forward, bringing my leg behind me and extending my arms backward to grab my ankle for the scorpion pose.

For the illusion, we stand in a V and bend our torsos toward the floor. In needle position, we move our bodies in a half circle, using the balls of our feet to propel us around. Our legs swing around, twirling like the hands of a pinwheel.

As we finish, the other dancers who've crowded into the studio applaud. Our contemp team links hands and takes a bow.

"Yeah, Sophie! Go, Gabby!" Grace, Brie, and Jada holler above everyone else.

I squeeze Sophie's hand. Grace, Brie, and Jada jump up and down as they cheer. They look so proud of us. I feel proud of myself too.

I finally figured it out. Old moves are just as important as new ones. Together they create something new and wonderful. Friends are the same. Bringing together old friends and new friends creates twice the fun and new memories.

ABOUT THE AUTHOR

Margaret Gurevich is the author of many books for kids, including Capstone's *Gina's Balance*, *Aerials and Envy*, and the award-winning Chloe by Design series. She has also written for *National Geographic Kids* and Penguin Young Readers. While Margaret hasn't done performance dance since she was a tween, this series has inspired her to take dance classes again. She lives in New Jersey with her son and husband.

ABOUT THE ILLUSTRATOR

Addy Rivera Sonda is a Mexican illustrator currently living in Los Angeles, California. She loves color and nature. They inspire her to think that stories and art are slowly but surely changing the way people understand themselves and perceive others, building empathy and a more inclusive world.

GLOSSARY

alignment (uh-LAHYN-muhnt)—the proper adjustment of parts in relation to each other

bristle (BRIS-uhl)—to show signs of anger

discipline (DIS-uh-plin)—a field of study

emphasize (EM-fuh-sahyz)—to stress as being important or so as to stand out

illusion (il-LOO-zhuhn)—a misleading image presented to the eye

latter (LAT-er)—the second of two things referred to

precise (pri-SAHYS)—very exact

propel (pruh-PEL)—to push or drive, usually forward or onward

rationally (ra-SHUH-nuh-lee)—having the ability to reason

unison (YOO-nuh-suhn)—in perfect agreement or at the same time

visualize (VIZH-oo-uh-lahyz)—to form a mental image of something

TALK ABOUT IT!

1. Trying something new, like Gabby does with contemporary dance, can be intimidating. Have you ever attempted something new? Were you nervous, excited, scared, etc.? Talk about how you felt.

2. Being the new kid in any situation can be hard. Imagine you are Sophie. Talk about how you would feel starting at a new dance school and not knowing anyone.

3. Both Gabby and her friends act poorly—talk about why you think each girl reacted the way she did. What are some of the possible reasons behind their feelings?

WRiTE ABOUT IT!

1. The disagreement in this story came from friends having different points of view. But what about Sophie's point of view? How do you think she felt during the scene at the mall? Write the scene in the dance store from her perspective.

2. All the dancers in this story specialize in different types of dance. If you could try one type of dance, what would it be? Write a paragraph explaining your choice.

3. Gabby and her friends have a tradition of getting pizza after ballet practice. Do you and your friends have any traditions? Pick one and write a paragraph explaining what it is and why it's special.

MORE ABOUT CONTEMPORARY DANCE

Contemporary dance is a type of dance that combines elements of several other disciplines, including classical, modern, jazz, and ballet. Contemporary was first created in the mid-20th century and is still popular today.

Although contemporary dance emphasizes the strong, controlled legwork of ballet, it also allows dancers to be creative and improvise. Unlike the strict, precise movements of ballet, contemporary dancers work to connect the mind and body through fluid dance movements.

While many other types of dance require specific footwear—like ballet slippers or tap shoes— contemporary dance is often done barefoot. It can also be performed to many different types of music. Contemp dancers often focus on floorwork, using gravity to pull them down to the floor. Unpredictable changes in rhythm, speed, and direction are also a part of contemporary style.